The Ugly Little Swan

James Riordan
Illustrated by Henning Löhlein

A & C Black • London

White Wolves series consultant: Sue Ellis,
Centre for Literacy in Primary Education

This book can be used in the White Wolves Guided Reading
programme by readers who need a lot of support in Year 2

First published 2009 by
A & C Black Publishers Ltd
36 Soho Square, London, W1D 3QY

www.acblack.com

Text copyright © 2009 James Riordan
Illustrations copyright © 2009 Henning Löhlein

The rights of James Riordan and Henning Löhlein to be identified
as the author and illustrator of this work has been asserted by them
in accordance with the Copyrights, Designs and Patents Act 1988.

ISBN 978-1-4081-1378-3

A CIP catalogue for this book is available from the British Library.

This book is produced using paper that is made from wood
grown in managed, sustainable forests. It is natural, renewable
and recyclable. The logging and manufacturing processes conform
to the environmental regulations of the country of origin.

Printed and bound in China

Chapter One

Mother swan was waiting for her eggs to hatch.

Crack-crack.

One head came out.

Then two…

three…

four…

five.

"Are you all here?" said Mother swan.

No! One little egg was left.

"Come on, hurry up!" she said.

Crack-crack.

At last, the little egg burst.

A head came out.

"Pak-pak," it said.

Mother swan was surprised.

"It's not like the others," she said.

"It's small and brown and *ugly!*"

Chapter Two

The ugly little swan wanted to play.
But the other babies chased him away.
"You're not like us," they hissed.
"Go and play on your own."

The little swan was sad.

The big swans pecked him.

An angry dog barked at him.

Even his father chased him off.

"He's so *ugly*," they all said.
At last, the little swan went away.

Chapter Three

The little swan hadn't gone far when…

Whoosh!

Two wild geese flew down.

"Come with us and see the world," they said.

Suddenly, a gun went off.

BANG! BANG!

It scared the geese away.

The little swan carried on.
Soon he came to a hut. An old
woman lived there with a cat and a hen.

The little swan went inside.

The old woman was very happy.

"Now I'll have swan eggs!" she cried.

But the cat and the hen were cross.

"Can you purr?" asked the cat.

"No," said the little swan.

"Can you lay eggs?" asked the hen.
"I don't think so," said the little swan.

"Then we don't want you here," they
said. "Go away!"

Chapter Four

The little swan was all alone again.
He made his home on a lake.

The months passed...
Autumn came and the air grew cold.

One evening, the little swan saw a
group of birds fly up from the lake.

Some had fluffy white feathers, some
had shiny green heads and yellow beaks.

They were ducks, flying to warmer
lands across the sea.

What beautiful birds, thought the
little swan.

He could not forget them.

Autumn and winter passed…

Spring came and the sun shone again.
Suddenly, some ducks landed on the
lake. They dipped below the water and
shook their feathers.

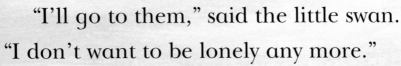

"I'll go to them," said the little swan.
"I don't want to be lonely any more."

Chapter Five

The little swan swam towards the ducks.
He dropped his head, and what did
he see? *Himself*!

But he was no longer an ugly little bird. Now he had a rich brown body, a beautiful green head and a yellow beak. He was not a swan – he was a *duck*!

A boy and a girl ran up.

"Look!" cried the boy. "The ducks are back."

They threw bread into the water.

"And there's a new one!" said the girl.
"Isn't he lovely?"

The little bird shook his feathers and stretched his beautiful green neck.

How proud he felt.

He was so happy to be a duck!